ARVIND

The Mind That Couldn't Be Weaponised

ARVIND

The Mind That Couldn't Be Weaponised

DEVI SINGH RAGHUVANSHI

Anecdote
Publishing House
For the love of quality reading!

Anecdote
Publishing House
For the love of quality reading!

anecdotepublishinghouse.com
champreaders.com

Anecdote Publishing House
2nd Floor 2/15 Lane no. 2 Ansari Road, Daryaganj-110002
Email: info@anecdotepublishinghouse.com
Website: anecdotepublishinghouse.com

Published by Anecdote Publishing House

First Edition 2026
ISBN 978-81-988015-2-4
MRP ₹ 350

Book Promoted and Marketed by Champ Readers Pvt. Ltd.
Editor: Meraki
Cover design by: Rishikumar Thakur
Layout by: Arivazhagi Balasundaram
Printed in India

DEDICATION

Dedicated to my Parents who made me read and write, even though they were just farmers.

This book is also dedicated to those who embody a deep sense of duty and selflessness—placing the needs of others above their own—which leads to true fulfilment and lasting happiness. The author is neither a nuclear scientist nor an authority on Hinduism; therefore, any errors or misinterpretations may kindly be regarded as part of the narrativc.

ACKNOWLEDGEMENTS

I gratefully acknowledge and express my heartfelt thanks to my wife, Sushma, for her valuable input, meticulous spell checks, and—most importantly—the inspiration and ideas I drew from observing the depth of her patience.

My elder daughter, Preeti, deserves special thanks for her contribution of content resources and for the emotional and financial support that made the publication of this book possible.

To my younger daughter, Payal, I extend my warm invitation to be a true partner in this endeavour. I must admit—quite frankly—that I have drawn freely from some of her blogs to enrich the content and make this book more authentic.

My sincere thanks also go to Mr Rajesh Chaurasia, my colleague, for patiently typing the entire manuscript.

I am especially grateful to all my friends on Facebook and my college mates, whose encouragement motivated me to undertake this writing journey.

Last but certainly not least, my heartfelt thanks would be incomplete without acknowledging the profound guidance of the *Bhagavad Gita* and the ever-resourceful *Google*.

Each one of you—whether your contribution was big or small—has been an essential part of this effort.

DISCLAIMER

The contents of this book are entirely the product of the author's imagination. Any resemblance to actual names, places, or incidents is purely coincidental and unintentional.

The author accepts no responsibility for any loss or damage arising from the publication of this book. However, he expresses sincere regret for any unintended harm that may occur.

1

Arvind Rangnathan was born in a small village in Tamil Nadu where his father, T. K. Ramaswamy, a primary school teacher, instilled in him a deep love for learning. Despite all the odds of a conservative society, an age-old system of caste discrimination and most importantly despite financial struggles, Arvind's father made sure he had access to books and nurtured his curiosity in science and mathematics.

In that ambience of poverty, Arvind would often sit under the dim light of a kerosene lamp, solving complex problems far beyond his grade level. The people around him often asked challenging science and mathematics questions just to embarrass him, but he calmly answered them all, much to their astonishment. His composure and knowledge earned him the respect of both the older generation and his young friends.

It is true that God helps those who help themselves. His exceptional talent became evident when Arvind, at the age of 11, made a diesel pump using scrap material to irrigate his school garden. This innovation brought him to limelight. This caught the attention of Shri Sampath Giri, his village head and the principal of his school,

K. Vishwanathan who helped him secure a scholarship to a prestigious high school in Chennai. However, adjusting to a new environment was tough. His classmates came from affluent backgrounds and he often faced ridicule for his modest upbringing.

Undeterred Arvind immersed himself in physics, inspired by legends like Dr. C. V. Raman and Dr. Homi Bhabha. His breakthrough came when he won a national science competition for developing an innovative cooling system using all green environment friendly material, earning a scholarship to study at the Indian Institute of Technology, Chennai.

He completed his graduation from IIT Chennai, but his ambitions lay elsewhere — in the field of nuclear science. As luck favours the brave, Arvind got the opportunity to pursue his Master's in Nuclear Science at the Indian Institute of Science (IISc), Bangalore.

Unfortunately, Arvind's father expired leaving a big vacuum in his life. He brought his mother, Nirmala Rameshwaram with him to a small rented accommodation. This event deeply impacted Arvind, intensifying his inner turmoil. Losing his father created an emotional and financial strain, forcing him to take full responsibility for his mother. Despite his devotion to Lord Krishna and his passion for nuclear physics, he struggled to manage his newfound responsibilities.

Bringing his mother to a small rented accommodation, Arvind tried to balance his studies and spiritual pursuits while ensuring her well-being. His mother, grieving the loss of her husband found solace in prayers and rituals, further strengthening Arvind's belief that divine intervention had guided him through his darkest times. However, the burden of managing household expenses, pursuing his research, and staying committed to his spiritual path often pushed him to the brink.

At times he questioned whether he could fulfil all his duties. Would his faith and knowledge be enough to overcome these challenges or would his inner conflicts consume him?

At IISc, Arvind's brilliance in nuclear physics set him apart, however, financial constraints forced him to often skip meals and he worked as a part time tutor to many children of the faculties. One professor, Shri Gopalan, father of one of his students recognised his potential and recommended him as his research associate and also for a government fellowship which enabled him to pursue his own research in nuclear fission and reactor construction.

Despite facing bureaucratic hurdles and resistance from senior scientists who doubted his abilities due to his modest background. The first rebuttal or challenge came from his immediate superior when Arvind suggested to reduce the thickness of the reactor wall by using his own innovative cooling. Arvind suggested using a more efficient refrigerant for faster and economical cooling of the reactor process. He was lampooned by Mr. Krishnamurthy, who sarcastically rejected his idea by pointing out that the reactors are serious consideration for their construction and no compromise could be done by reducing the thickness of that concrete enclosure. According to him, Arvind's suggestion was rejected outright by fear of radiation leakage. Arvind was not disappointed and remained focused. His research on controlled nuclear chain reactions earned him an opportunity to work with India's leading Nuclear Scientists at Bhabha Atomic Research Centre (BARC) in Mumbai.

At BARC, Arvind worked on India's peaceful Nuclear Energy programme contributing to the development of Advanced Reactor Technology. His innovations in nuclear fuel efficiency gained him international recognition and he was known as one of the youngest scientists to lead a major research division. He became a known name in nuclear physics worldwide.

2

Usha Bhatnagar, a young and ambitious associate in the same research facility, had been observing Arvind for quite some time. Unlike most of their colleagues who indulged in casual conversations and occasional outings, Arvind remained engrossed in his research, rarely engaging in social interaction. His deep inclination towards Nuclear Physics and his quiet spiritual reflections made him standout from the rest. Though not conventionally handsome, there was something intriguing about him, perhaps the intense focus in his eyes, the quiet confidence with which he carried himself or the rare moments when he spoke with profound clarity about his work and beliefs.

Usha was naturally drawn to intelligent minds and Arvind's peculiar mix of scientific brilliance and spiritual inclination piqued her curiosity. At first, she had merely observed him from a distance but as days passed, she found herself wanting to know more about him. Why was he always so detached? Did he ever feel the need for companionship? And most importantly, what lay beneath that silent demeanour?

One afternoon, as Arvind sat alone in the library, flipping through a book on quantum mechanics, Usha decided to break the ice. Gathering her courage, she approached him with a smile and said, "Arvind, I see you always lost in your thoughts. Ever thought of taking a break?"

Arvind looked up, slightly surprised and after a pause replied, "Break? From what?" His response wasn't dismissive, but rather a genuine inquiry, as if he truly didn't see the need for one. This only intrigued Usha further.

Usha chuckled at Arvind's response. She pulled out a chair and sat across from him.

"From work, from numbers, from equations, you know the usual things that makes life monotonous?"

Arvind closed his book halfway, his fingers still resting on the pages, "But if work gives me peace, why should I take a break from it?" His tone wasn't defensive, just genuinely inquisitive. Usha tilted her head, studying him. "Does work give you peace, or is it an escape from something else?"

Arvind's gaze flickered for a moment, as if the question had struck a hidden chord. He leaned back, his eyes momentarily drifting towards the large window beside them, where the evening Sun cast long shadows across the floor. "Work is my prayer Usha. Every equation, every discovery brings me closer to understanding the universe, I find glimpses of the divine."

Usha smiled, intrigued, "So physics is your way of reaching god?"

Arvind nodded slightly, "Something like that. I believe science and spirituality are not separate. They are two sides of the same truth."

Arvind gave a small thoughtful smile. "Perhaps, but I haven't given it much thought. My path has always been different."

Usha rested her chin on her hand, fascinated, "That's an interesting perspective. But don't you think human connections, friendships, maybe even love, are also part of that truth?"

Usha wasn't sure why, but she felt a strange pull towards this man, who spoke of science and spirituality as if they were both one. He wasn't arrogant nor dismissive — just deeply absorbed in his own world and for the first time she wanted to step into that world and understand.

Arvind held Usha's gaze for a moment longer than necessary. Something about her words lingered in his mind. He wasn't used to such conversations. Most people either admired his intellect from a distance or dismissed him as someone too lost in his own world. But Usha… she was just different. She wasn't merely curious, she was challenging his perspective and making him question his own detachment.

For the first time in a long while, Arvind felt a shift within him, an unfamiliar warmth, a pull towards something beyond equations and cosmic theories.

Usha noticed the subtle change in his expression. A tiny crack had appeared in the fortress he had built around himself. She decided to push a little further. "Tell me something Arvind. Have you ever wondered what it feels like to share your thoughts with someone? Not just in a research paper or a lecture but in a personal way, with someone who truly listens?"

Arvind hesitated. His mind instinctively sought logical reasoning but his heart — an entity he had long kept in check — whispered a different answer. "Maybe I never found the right person who would listen," he admitted, his voice quieter than before.

Usha's lips curled into a gentle smile. "Maybe you just never looked."

And with that the first spark was ignited. A spark that neither of them fully understood yet, but one that had the potential to turn into something much bigger – something that could change both of their lives.

3

Arvind was struggling with emotions because of his deep spiritual inclination and his focus on nuclear physics. His emotional struggle was evident as it was leading him to an affair but he wasn't sure whether Usha shared a similar spiritual or intellectual connection with him. In that case, their bond could remain platonic, yet deeply meaningful. For Arvind, this relationship was taking a more complex turn. He was exploring his internal conflict — his devotion to spirituality versus the temptation of a romantic or emotional affair.

He was in deep dilemma. If Usha becomes a source of emotional support during his struggle, their connection could intensify leading to a serious moral dilemma. After a careful examination of his heart and mind, Arvind preferred it to remain a purely intellectual and emotional bond.

Their internal struggle between heart, mind and bodily desires was adding a great depth to their relationship but so far, they had consciously decided to remain in platonic love, their journey was revolving around resisting temptations while acknowledging their human emotions.

Arvind being spiritually inclined was trying to justify their bond as pure devotion, seeing Usha as a divine presence in his life. However, he became apprehensive during moments of intense attraction that could shake his beliefs, making him question, whether suppressing natural desires was truly the right path.

Their shared intellectual pursuits could keep them deeply connected but moments of vulnerability – such as personal losses, loneliness or deep conversations could blur the boundaries between platonic and romantic love.

They both sat together and drew an unspoken agreement and according to this they would never explicitly cross the line. They both knew that their unspoken longing for each other could create an emotional turmoil where they would oscillate between restraint and surrender. In moments of extreme emotional intensity, they both faltered, only to retreat and reaffirm their decision to remain platonic.

Arvind was constantly facing scepticism from his scientific peers who were dismissing his spiritual beliefs, while traditionalists were questioning his deep involvement in nuclear physics. Behind their backs, they were rumours of an illicit relationship between Usha and him and some of them even compared them to "Beauty and the Beast".

Arvind never knew how he would navigate these opposing forces that could shape his characters' growth. Both Usha and Arvind decided to prove that science and spirituality could co-exist. Arvind's existential question,

"Why am I here in this world", was becoming the driving force behind his dual quest for scientific and spiritual truth.

With all his possible source of strength and knowledge, he started exploring both physics and spirituality as complementary to each other. Usha supported him in this quest.

4

Arvind's relentless dedication and deep passion for nuclear physics earned him numerous national and international accolades. His groundbreaking research in nuclear fusion and radiation safety led to prestigious awards. He had even sacrificed his research on reducing the thickness of the reactor wall from 1 metre to 0.750 metre by improving the reactor's cooling system, keeping in mind the advice and concerns of senior scientists regarding possible radiation leakage. Yet, his prestigious awards included:

1) Recognition for his pioneering work in sustainable nuclear energy and quantum mechanics at the national level.
2) International honours for his contributions to theoretical nuclear physics and quantum mechanics.
3) The Padma Bhushan, awarded by the Government of India in acknowledgment of his exceptional achievements in science and technology.
4) The Global Energy Innovation Award, presented for his advancements in nuclear fusion as a future energy source.

5) A nomination for the Nobel Prize, owing to his groundbreaking work in nuclear safety and radiation shielding.

ᘓᘐ ᘓᘐ ᘓᘐ

Despite his success, Arvind kept himself from being too proud and behaved always to maintain his modesty while being spiritually connected to Lord Krishna and attributing all his achievements to divine blessings. His life became an extraordinary blend of devotion and scientific brilliance.

When asked by the media, "Who do you attribute these achievements to?" he replied, "Whatever I have discovered is merely a reflection of the divine order of the universe. Science is my karma, and devotion is my soul."

His unique ability to merge rational scientific thought with spiritual wisdom made him a rare figure in the scientific community—one who inspired both physicists and spiritual seekers alike.

5

As Arvind's career in nuclear physics flourished, his personal life was a complex interplay of intense scientific pursuit, deep spiritual devotion and moments of solitude. His journey was filled with sacrifices, inner conflicts and profound realisation that shaped his identity beyond science. His passion for physics left him with little time for personal relationships. However, he did fall in an affair with Usha, who admired his intellect and dedication.

Arvind and Usha's love was like an unfinished melody – felt deeply but never spoken aloud. It was there in the way they looked at each other in the silent pauses of their conversations and in the warmth of their unspoken words. There was unspoken love between them.

Arvind and Usha often met during scientific conferences and spiritual gatherings, both drawn to the mysteries of the universe — one through nuclear physics, the other through philosophy.

One evening, as Arvind was explaining the concept of nuclear fusion, Usha listened intently. But she wasn't absorbing the science; she was watching the passion in his eyes, the way his hands moved, the way his voice carried both conviction and gentleness.

When he finished, their eyes met. Usha smiled softly and said, "You talk about atoms uniting but do you ever wonder about souls merging?"

Arvind hesitated. Instead, he just smiled back. Neither of them said the words but in the moment, they both knew.

They would text each other. Sometimes it was about science, sometimes about Krishna's philosophy and sometimes about nothing at all.

One night Usha messaged: *If love had a frequency, what would it be?*

Arvind replied: *It would be the resonance of two souls vibrating at the same energy level without saying a word.*

Usha read his message and closed her eyes, feeling his presence in the silence.

One afternoon, as they were walking together in a temple courtyard, Arvind was explaining the cosmic significance of Lord Krishna and Usha listened with all her heart. She suddenly stopped, turned and asked, "Arvind, have you ever felt something so deeply but never had the courage to say it?" He looked at her, understanding the weight of her words. He said, "Some things are better left unsaid, Usha.... because once spoken, they lose their purity." She nodded but, in her heart, she wished, he would break his own rule just once.

Arvind had to leave for a long research assignment abroad. The night before his departure, Usha found an envelope tucked inside her favourite book.

It was a letter from Arvind.

Dear Usha,

Some equations are incomplete, some stories remain unfinished, our is one such story. But know this – if parallel universe exists, then in one of them, I have already told you how much you mean to me. And in another you already know.

Tears welled in her eyes. She pressed the letter against her heart and whispered, "I always knew, Arvind …. I always knew."

Their love was felt not declared. It was in stolen glances, half-finished sentences and the spaces between their words. Even in separation, they carried each other like an eternal vibration of energy — never fading, never lost.

Usha knew that this relationship with Arvind was being built on intense intellectual conversations. Usha admired his dedication, but at the back of her mind, she was often worried about his erratic behaviour and tendency to detach from the world. While she believed in love as a stabilising force, Arvind saw it as another challenge in his spiritual and scientific journey.

6

Arvind's lecture on nuclear fusion in the U.S. was a turning point in his career. Scientists, researchers and policymakers from all over the world had gathered for the event, eager to hear his insights. His ability to blend cutting edge nuclear physics with ancient Hindu wisdom made his presentation one of the most unique and compelling sessions of the conference.

As he spoke, the audience was captivated by his depth of knowledge and his unconventional approach. He not only explained the technicalities of fusion energy but also emphasised its philosophical significance, comparing the energy of the universe to the balance between creation and destruction much like Lord Shiva's cosmic dance.

During the Q&A session, Arvind was asked about the ethical implications of Fusion Energy and how spirituality influenced his scientific pursuits. He responded by emphasising that true knowledge is never separate from morality and that science, when guided by wisdom can lead to universal well-being.

His lecture received a standing ovation and many experts in the field approached him afterwards to discuss future collaboration. This moment reinforced Arvind's belief that his path – one of both devotion and discovery was leading him exactly where he was meant to be. Representatives from top institutions in Europe, Japan and the Middle East expressed their desire to work with him on international projects. Even government agencies showed interest in his ideas, seeing him as a visionary who could bridge science and ethics in the pursuit of sustainable energy.

This overwhelming response filled Arvind with a deep sense of purpose. It was no longer just about physics but it was about guiding humanity toward a future where science and spirituality could coexist harmoniously. However, the sudden fame and attention also raised questions in his mind – *Was he ready for this global responsibility?*

Would his spiritual beliefs align with the practical demands of international scientific collaboration?

As Arvind returned to his hotel that night, he sat in deep contemplation. On one hand, this was everything he had ever worked for — recognition, collaboration and a real opportunity to shape the future of sustainable energy. On the other hand, he wondered if he was straying too far from this spiritual path. *Would being at the forefront of global nuclear research pull him away from his devotion to Lord Krishna?*

His mind drifted back to the moment that had changed his life. During his lowest financial state, he had prayed and miraculously received a scholarship. That moment had solidified his belief that everything happened according to divine will — Krishna's plan for him.

In the following weeks, Arvind was flooded with offers. Some projects focused on peaceful nuclear fusion for clean energy, while others had military implications, something that deeply disturbed him. At the same time, a leading European Research Institute invited him to lead a project on commercialising fusion energy which aligned perfectly with his ethical beliefs.

Torn between duty and devotion, Arvind visited a temple dedicated to Krishna before making his final decision. The realisation struck him. His duty was to contribute to the world and with newfound clarity, Arvind accepted the offer made by the European research institute. However, he imposed one condition — his research would never be used for destructive purpose. He embarked on this new journey.

Arvind settled into his role at the prestigious European research institute surrounded by some of the greatest minds in nuclear physics. The research environment was rigorous, demanding long hours of theoretical calculations, lab experiments and high-pressure meetings. Though his work was progressing satisfactorily, something felt incomplete.

Arvind soon realised that while he was achieving professional success, he was losing his inner peace.

Though Arvind still struggled at times, he now had a clear vision to develop fusion energy, not just as a scientist but as a seeker of truth. He was no longer just working on equation – he was contributing to a mission that aligned with both science and his soul. He started integrating his spiritual beliefs subtly into his work.

7

As Arvind delved deeper into his research at the European institute, his schedule became even more demanding. Long hours in the lab, technical meetings and endless calculations left him exhausted. Yet, even in this state of extreme focus, something unexpected began to happen. He started dreaming about Usha. Usha was someone he had loved deeply without speaking and without expressing. She had been his silent supporter, understanding his struggles and aspirations. However, when he had left for the U.S. and then to Europe, he had done so without giving her any clear commitment about their future. In fact, at that time, he had convinced himself that his spiritual journey and scientific ambitions left no room for personal attachments.

But now, in his dreams, she appeared vividly, sometimes smiling, sometimes with eyes filled with unspoken questions. In one dream, she stood in a temple looking at him with an expression that seemed to ask, "Did I ever mean anything to you? Did you ever imagine us as husband and wife?"

Each time he woke up from these dreams, a strange sense of longing and guilt filled him. *Had he been unfair to Usha? Had he abandoned something precious in pursuit of knowledge and devotion?* Arvind tried to suppress these thoughts, convincing himself that his spiritual and scientific path was more important than his personal relationships. But the dreams persisted, becoming more frequent especially during moments of extreme stress.

Now Arvind faced a new dilemma — should he reach out to Usha after all these years, or had too much time passed?

Questions haunted his mind. Was she married or dating anyone? Was she still working with BARC? Would she even want to hear from him? And if she did, what would he say?

He realised that just as he had been trying to balance science and spirituality, he now had to confront something as complex – the unresolved emotions of his past. He would now be dealing with his biggest inner turmoil. He would certainly try to find Usha rather than being "Let the past remain in the past".

8

After completing his tenure at the European Research Institute, Arvind returned to India, carrying a heavy heart. His research had been successful, but the deep void within him remained. The dreams of Usha had not stopped and he knew that he had to confront his past.

With a mixture of nervousness and hope, he decided to visit Usha's house. He imagined countless possibilities; would she still be waiting for him? Would she be angry? Would she have moved on? But nothing prepared him for what he discovered.

Usha was married. And not just to anyone. She was now the wife of Professor S. Chakrapani, the Head of the Department of Nuclear Science at IIT Bombay. Arvind felt a rush of conflicting emotions. He was happy for Usha as she had found a partner who shared her intellectual world, someone who could appreciate her brilliance. Yet, the news crushed him. A deep guilt settled in his heart. He had left her without closure, without a promise and now it was too late.

He stood outside her house, unable to move. He didn't have the courage to knock on the door. Instead, he sat on a bench nearby, staring at the ground, lost in his thoughts.

"I was the one who walked away, she deserved better than waiting for someone who never had any answer and not even a hope."

Memories of Usha flooded his mind, her soft laughter, the way she had supported him silently, her patient understanding of his struggles. He realised, he had been selfish, thinking only about his own journey, his own conflicts between science and spirituality, without considering how much he had hurt her.

The guilt was unbearable. He wanted to run away from the pain, but he also knew that he had to face it.

"Should I at least meet her once? Apologise for leaving without a word?" he wondered.

But what right did he have to interfere in her life now? She was married, settled and possibly happy. His presence might only bring back pain.

After sitting in turmoil for hours, Arvind made his decision — he would not disturb Usha's life.

As he was about to leave and bid a silent goodbye, Usha caught a glimpse of him through her kitchen window. She ran towards him and tried to speak to him but Arvind as usual in a hurry and guilt disappeared from her sight.

He took out his notebook and wrote a heartfelt letter, not to send to her but to unburden his soul.

Usha,

I was a fool. I thought, I was choosing knowledge and devotion but I was running from the person who truly understood me. I left without a word thinking that the detachment was the answer, not realising that I was breaking a heart that never deserved such silence. Today I stand outside your world, happy for you, yet shattered by my own guilt. I wish I had been braver, wiser. But if I have lost the right to say these words to you, let them at least find peace within me. You deserve all the happiness in the world. I will carry this regret but I will never let it touch your life again.

Arvind

With a deep sigh, he folded the letter and put it back in his pocket. He looked at Usha's house one last time, whispered a silent prayer for her happiness and walked away — carrying the weight of love, loss and an unspoken farewell.

9

As Arvind walked away from Usha's house, the weight of regret sat heavily on his chest. The realisation that he had been unfair to Usha and leaving without closure haunted him. He returned to his own quiet world, but something inside him had changed. For weeks, he struggled with a deep sadness. His research, once his greatest passion, now felt empty. His prayers and meditations, which once gave him strength, now brought a painful awareness of his own failures. He had spent his life balancing science and spirituality, but he had neglected the most fundamental aspect of existence – human relationships.

Arvind immersed himself in work, hoping that research would distract him from the emotional storm within. He started giving guest lectures, engaging in new projects and mentoring young scientists. But every time he saw a couple walking together, or heard a familiar song —Usha's face would flash before him.

He often found himself revisiting old letters and memories, wondering, *Had I stayed, would things have been different? Was my pursuit of knowledge worth losing love?*

He knew there were no answers; only lessons.

As somebody has said, "Tragedies do not come alone." means that when one misfortune occurs, it is often followed by a series of other negative events, essentially stating that bad things tend to happen in clusters.

Just as Arvind was trying to come to terms with Usha's absence from his life, another tragedy struck – his mother passed away.

She had always been his anchor, the one person who understood his struggles between spirituality and science. Whenever he was lost, she would gently remind him, "Arvind, knowledge is powerful, but without love and companionship, it is incomplete."

Her last words to him before she took her final breath were, "Arvind, you have given so much to the world but what have you given to yourself? Find someone who will walk with you. Don't spend your life in solitude. It is not what I want for you."

Her plea echoed in his mind long after she was gone. He had already lost Usha and now he had lost the one person who truly cared for him unconditionally. For months after his mother's passing, Arvind felt completely lost. He buried himself in work, trying to escape the emptiness in his heart. But this loss was different.

Losing Usha was painful, but it had been his own doing. Losing his mother, however felt like a punishment from fate. It was a cruel reminder that — time waits for no one.

For the first time, he questioned his choices deeply. Had he misunderstood his spiritual path? Had he denied himself happiness under the illusion of detachment? Was it too late to change?

One day, while looking through his mother's belongings, he found an old letter she had written, for him long ago. In it she had written,

Arvind, you are my pride. I know you are meant for great things. But a great life is not just about achievements, it is about shared moments, love and finding someone who can be your companion in both knowledge and faith. When I am gone, promise me you won't close your heart forever.

Tears welled in his eyes, this was not just his mother's wish, it was her final blessing for him. For the first time, he allowed himself to think.

"Is it possible to start again? Could I find love, not to replace Usha, but to honour my mother's wish?"

Arvind stood at the crossroads of duty and despair, torn between his mother's last wish and the unbearable weight of his own shattered soul. Life had already dealt him two merciless blows, leaving him hollow stripped of confidence and uncertain of his own place in the world. And now just when he needed solitude, fate burdened him with yet another expectation — a family responsibility, he wasn't sure he could honour.

His mother had always believed in the strength of relationships, in the unbreakable fabric of family bonds. He felt like an outsider in his own life, unable to trust himself with the weight another's dependence. He knew what was expected of him, yet the very thought of stepping into this new role suffocated him. Could he fulfil the duty he no longer felt connected to? Could he respect a relationship when he was struggling to respect his own existence?

Doubt clawed at his mind but walking away would mean betraying his mother's faith in him; staying would mean taking on a responsibility he wasn't sure he could carry. The choice wasn't just difficult, it was agonising. After endless nights of turmoil and self-reflection, Arvind finally arrived at a decision. He would not have another woman in his life. The thought of a new relationship, one that his family expected him to accept, felt like a betrayal to the love and memories he still carried within him. Usha wasn't just a person from his past, she was the essence of his deepest emotions, the only woman who had ever truly touched his soul.

He knew what his family wanted. They saw his loneliness, his broken state and believed that a new relationship might heal him. But they didn't understand, his wounds weren't the kind that time or companionship could mend. Some losses carve themselves too deeply into a man's heart, leaving behind scars that no one else can smooth over.

Arvind wasn't better nor did he resent the expectations placed upon him. He simply knew the truth — he had loved once completely and irrevocably. And for him, that love was enough for a lifetime.

10

The grand hall of IIT Bombay buzzed with intellectual discussions on nuclear advancements. Renowned scientists and scholars gathered for the event but one name on the speaker list stood out — Dr. Arvind Rangnathan — once a rising star in nuclear physics, now more immersed in spirituality than research. After a long hiatus, Arvind had been invited by IIT Bombay to deliver a special lecture on *The Intersection of Nuclear Physics and Universal Energy*. Though he had stepped away from active research, his insights remained invaluable.

Arvind engrossed in a research presentation, casually turned his head and his breath caught. Across the room stood Usha, her eyes momentarily locking with his. Beside her was her husband, a well-dressed man, engaged in a conversation but noticing her sudden distraction.

Arvind was in a dilemma, feeling a pang of nostalgia, regret and unresolved emotions. He tried his best to maintain his spiritual detachment and focused on his purpose at the conference. Same way, Usha didn't expect to see Arvind and she also didn't know whether she was feeling awkward, happy or indifferent?

A hesitant smile formed on Usha's lips as she excused herself and walked towards Arvind. He straightened, feeling an odd mix of calmness and curiosity.

"Arvind… it's been years," she said softly.

"Indeed. And yet, the world keeps bringing us together — in the strangest way."

"I never thought I'd see you at a physics conference."

"Nuclear physics is my profession, but spirituality is my life. I suppose I'm balancing the two."

She tilted her head, genuinely intrigued. "Spirituality? I remember how passionate you were about it. Does it still guide your decisions?"

"More than ever. In fact, it has shaped the way I approach science. The universe and the divine — both follow profound laws of energy."

She studied him for a moment, "You seem …….. different more at peace." Just then her husband walked up, extending a firm handshake.

"Arvind, meet my husband, Dr. S. Chakrapani. He is the Head of the Department of Nuclear Science at IIT Bombay."

Arvind shook his hand "Oh, Dr. Chakrapani. I have read some of your research papers. Your work on nuclear fusion advancements is remarkable."

"Thank you, Dr. Arvind Rangnathan. Usha has mentioned your brilliance in physics before."

Arvind replied with a light chuckle, "I hope she only spoke of the physics part."

They all laughed, the tension melting away into something resembling closure.

As they parted ways, Arvind felt no sadness, no lingering 'what if' – just a quiet gratitude for a past that had shaped his present.

11

Everybody knew that Arvind was not committed to any institution. This had added an intriguing layer to Arvind Rangnathan's journey. His genius made him valuable not only to legitimate scientific institutions but also to rogue elements who wanted to exploit his knowledge for their own purposes. Arvind was never one to follow rigid instructions. His mind worked beyond the confines of structured learning and he often challenged authority when he found their methods inefficient. His independent thinking made him difficult figure to control but it also made him invaluable.

As he rose in the field of nuclear physics, various groups — governments, private defence contractors and even rogue elements wanted him on their side. They saw in him a man who could unlock the secrets of nuclear power for both peace and destruction.

Government of India's defence and energy departments after recognising his brilliance wanted him to lead classified nuclear projects. They saw his potential in advancing nuclear energy for civilian use but also in strengthening the country's nuclear defence strategy.

Foreign intelligence agencies and research labs of international powers tried to recruit him with lucrative offers, prestigious positions and research freedom. Some approached him officially, while others worked through covert means to lure him in.

The most dangerous offers came from shady organisations like Rogue Elements and Arms Dealers that dealt in nuclear weapons and black-market technology. They didn't just offer wealth but they threatened him. These groups understood that if they couldn't recruit Arvind, eliminating him might be next option. Throughout history, scientists have faced abductions and assassinations, often due to sensitive nature of their works and geopolitical tensions.

Arvind never believed in war or destruction. He saw nuclear energy as a tool for scientific progress, energy independence and space exploration and not for annihilation. He also knew that his refusal to align with any one side made him a MAN IN DANGER.

He was in severe mental turmoil. Should he prioritise scientific freedom, or remain loyal to India's nuclear programme? Or should he simply pursue his research wherever he found the greatest intellectual liberty? Could he control how his discoveries would be used — or would they inevitably become weapons of mass destruction, regardless of his intentions?

Arvind's neutrality put him in a high stakes game where he was constantly watched, followed and even threatened. He had to outmanoeuvre spies, bureaucrats and criminals. When he rejected an offer from a powerful international defence conglomerate, he survived an assassination attempt in a "Mysterious Car Accident". The Indian intelligence agencies soon realised that protecting him was a national security priority not just for India's sake but for global stability.

Arvind eventually chose his own path refusing to work solely under any government or private institution. Instead, he formed his own independent research organisation, ensuring that his work remained focused on peaceful, ethical applications of nuclear technology. He mentored young scientists, creating a new generation that upheld his values. Despite constant pressure, his vision remained unshaken. He was a scientist, not a pawn in the geopolitical game.

But the world didn't forget him. He remained one of the most watched men on the planet, walking the fine line between scientific freedom and political power.

Arvind Rangnathan's life was no longer just about a man who rose to scientific greatness but it was about a man who stood firm in a world where everyone wanted to control him. His life became a thrilling battle of intelligence, survival and ethical dilemma — making him both an inspiration and a target.

12

As Arvind Rangnathan's influence in the nuclear world grew, so did the threats against him. Various global powers and shady organisation wanted his mind and when persuasion failed, one group took a drastic step of abduction. He was attending a high-profile nuclear energy summit at Taj Palace, New Delhi, where he was set to deliver a speech on India's future in thorium-based nuclear energy. Security was tight but unknown to the Indian authorities, rogue elements from the Middle East had already infiltrated the city.

On the night before his presentation, as Arvind stepped out to take a private call, he was suddenly surrounded by armed men dressed as security personnel. Before he could react, a needle pricked his neck — a tranquilliser. His world faded to black and he was abducted by using a VIP car.

Arvind woke up in a dark cargo container, hands and legs bound, the cold steel pressing against his skin. The container was moving and he was being smuggled out of India. Through the faint cracks, he heard conversations in Pashto and Arabic. His captors were likely from Middle Eastern arms syndicate, operating between Pakistan and Afghanistan. After what seemed like days, the container was finally opened. Arvind was dragged into a mountainous compound deep within the Afghanistan-Pakistan border region, a strong hold of nuclear black-market dealers.

A tall, imposing man with a deep scar on his cheek stepped forward.

"Welcome Dr.Rangnathan," he said in a heavy Arabic accent, "you will help us, or you will die here."

Arvind was then imprisoned in a heavily guarded underground bunker. His captors were led by Sheikh Khaled Al-Nasser, a feared arms dealer who supplied nuclear material to rogue states and terrorist groups.

"India refuses to use its nuclear brilliance for power. We will use your knowledge for something greater — control over nations," Khaled declared.

Actually, they wanted Arvind to refine nuclear warheads stolen from old Soviet stockpiles and to create a portable nuclear device that could be smuggled into cities undetected. If he refused, they threatened to hand him over to foreign intelligence agencies, who would torture him for secrets—or worse, kill him and frame it as a failure of Indian Intelligence.

But Arvind was not just a scientist, he was a strategist. Arvind pretended to cooperate asking for access to computers lab equipment and technical books. He knew that stalling was his best defence.

Over the next three weeks, he fed them false research designed to delay their nuclear ambitions. At the same time, he secretly embedded a distress signal within the technical files, hoping that an Indian Intelligence agency would intercept it. Most daring of all, he managed to turn one of the warlord's tech experts — Anya, a disillusioned scientist — into an ally.

One night Anya revealed a critical piece of intel.

"You are marked for execution, once they have enough from you. They will kill you."

They had to act fast.

Using a faulty circuit in the bunker's security system, Arvind and Anya caused a power outage, throwing the compound into darkness.

Under the cover of chaos, they disabled the guards by using tranquillisers that were stolen by Anya. They also stole military jeep and raced toward the nearest Pakistani border town.

By this time, Indian Intelligence and RAW (Research & Analysis Wing) had intercepted Arvind's distress signal and along with U.S. agencies, launched a covert rescue operation.

As Khaled's men closed in on the escapes, a drone strike obliterated the strong hold, erasing the rogue syndicates nuclear ambitions.

Arvind was secretly flown back to India, where his survival was kept classified to avoid diplomatic tensions.

The Pakistani and Afghan governments denied any knowledge of the syndicate, calling it a terrorist faction acting independently.

Anya defected to India, joining Arvind's research team to counter nuclear black-market threats.

Despite being free Arvind realised his life would never be the same again. Arvind Rangnathan had returned home but the man who stepped back into India was not the same one who had been abducted. Despite being celebrated as a NATIONAL HERO, his mind was a battlefield of confusion, paranoia and deep existential stress.

Even in the safety of his home, Arvind felt watched. Every shadow seemed like a lurking threat. Every stranger in a crowd felt like a potential abductor. The nightmares never stopped and visions of being dragged through tunnels, the cold metal of a gun against his temple, the chilling voice of Sheikh Khaled whispering, "YOU WILL NEVER BE FREE" haunted him. More than that, the moral conflict tormented him.

He had seen the hunger for nuclear power in dangerous hands — how easily his knowledge could be twisted into a weapon of mass destruction. Yet, he had also witnessed the helplessness of his own country, which relied on intelligence agencies to save him rather than harnessing its own technological prowess.

Arvind had once dreamed of a peaceful nuclear revolution of energy, prosperity and India's rise as a technological giant but now he doubted everything. When he returned to his lab, he found himself unable to focus. Equations that once excited him now felt pointless.

He was consumed by wild thoughts. What if my research is used to build the very weapons, I fought to stop? What if another group abducts me? What if I don't escape next time? Can my government truly protect me or am I just a pawn in a larger game?

The burden of his own genius became his greatest curse.

Arvind began withdrawing from public life. He rejected interviews, refused to attend global conferences and limited his interactions to only a handful of trusted colleagues.

His home was now guarded 24/7, but even that didn't make him feel safe. He suspected his phone was tapped, his emails monitored not just by foreign agencies but by his own government. He refused to take any classified projects, fearing they might make him an even bigger target.

His extended family and colleagues noticed the change. His once sharp mind now hesitated. His once confident speeches were now filled with doubt. Even Anya, the woman who had helped him escape, saw the change in him.

"You saved yourself, but you are still trapped Arvind, you have to choose, live or just exist in fear."

One evening, while working late in his lab, he received an unmarked envelope. Inside was a single piece of paper with a handwritten message, "WE ARE STILL WATCHING. THE GAME ISN'T OVER."

His hands trembled as he clutched the note. The air around him grew suffocating. He felt like, he was back in that bunker, chained and helpless. *Was it a real threat or just his paranoia?*

He didn't know.

Arvind's escape did not bring him peace. He lived in a world where he couldn't trust anyone, not even his own government. He couldn't pursue his dreams, fearing that they might be used against humanity.

Throughout Arvind Rangnathan had been a man of logic, science and reason but now he was a shadow of his former self, a brilliant mind that had been pushed to the edge and broken beyond repair.

Arvind's detachment became more severe each day as he spoke less and less, often staring into empty space for hours. He stopped reading research papers or even engaging in scientific discussions. Nuclear physics — once his passion, now felt meaningless. He showed no excitement, no anger, not even fear. It was as if emotions had been erased.

His students and colleagues whispered, "He is here, but not really here." He had become an outsider in his own world. His sister held his hands and wept pleading, "Arvind, come back to us. You are safe now." But his gaze remained hollow, distant as if she was a stranger. Anya, the woman who had helped him escape, visited him and said, "You fought so hard to survive, but now you are letting them win."

Arvind just smiled vaguely as if he didn't understand what she was saying. He also stopped caring about money, recognition, and even survival. He no longer felt human desires. Slowly, he became a recluse.

He would walk alone at night, barefoot, mumbling equations to himself. He started talking to the air, as if debating with invisible people. Some nights, he sat on the rooftop for hours, staring at the sky, whispering — *there is nothing left to achieve, nothing left to understand.*

14

As his mental state declined, Arvind began seeing and hearing things that weren't there. He heard Khaled's voice in his head mocking him, "You think you escaped, but you are my prisoner." He saw numbers floating in the air, equations that made no sense. He had visions of nuclear explosions, burning the world into ashes. HIS MIND WAS COLLAPSING.

One evening, his students found him sitting in the middle of a busy road, laughing softly. A truck came speeding towards him but he didn't move. He just kept staring at the headlights, mesmerised, as if waiting to be consumed by the light. At the last moment, a passerby pulled him away, but Arvind didn't thank him. He simply sighed and whispered, "I don't belong here anymore." The passerby admitted him to a nearby mental asylum.

The man who had once deciphered the mysteries of the atom, now found himself locked inside a mental hospital.

The passerby who saved him had assumed he was a lunatic, trying to kill himself. The police, unable to identify him, sent him to a state-run psychiatric hospital.

The ward smelled of disinfectant and despair. The corridors echoed with the incoherent mumblings of the lost souls who lived there.

Arvind, once a man who had debated nuclear policy with world leaders, now sat cross-legged on the floor, drawing equations on the wall with a piece of chalk.

The doctors watched him curiously. He didn't scream, didn't attack anyone, he just spoke to people who weren't there. Sometimes, he debated with Einstein and Oppenheimer about nuclear ethics.

Sometimes, he argued with God, demanding to know why he had been given such a brilliant mind only to suffer. And sometimes, he sat in silence, staring at his own hands as if trying to remember what they were meant to do.

The world outside still remembered Arvind Rangnathan as India's greatest nuclear physicist. But within the walls of the mental asylum he was just another nameless patient, lost in the depths of his own mind. No one cared about his past achievements.

Every morning at 6:00am, a loud buzzer would wake up the patients. While others screamed, cried or refused to move, Arvind would quietly get up from his cot, walk to the wall and begin writing equations with his fingers.

Since no chalk was allowed, he used whatever he could find, a piece of a broken tile, charcoal from burnt paper or even his own blood if he had a wound.

The staff didn't bother stopping him. They assumed, he was writing nonsense. But one day, a junior psychiatrist noticed something strange.

"Doctor, look at this," he called out to his senior. "These aren't just random scribbles, they are complex nuclear physics formulas." The senior doctor merely shook his head. "It doesn't matter. He doesn't even know who he is anymore."

At lunch time the other patients would fight for food, curse at the nurses or sit in the corner, mumbling to themselves, but Arvind sat at the same spot, alone, having full-fledged conversations with invisible people. When the nurses tried to give him food, he would sometimes smile politely and accept it, other times he would refuse saying he didn't need material sustenance anymore.

As the sun set and the shadows grew longer, something would change in Arvind. His calmness would disappear. His eyes would dart around the room, as if he expecting someone to grab him. He would hug his knees, whispering in terror, "They're watching… they'll take me again…"

The doctors believed, it was paranoia — a symptom of PTSD. Sometimes, he would run to the door, banging on it violently, "Let me go out, they will come for me again."

The guards would inject him with a sedative until he collapsed back onto his cot, eyes rolling into his head.

The head psychiatrist, Dr. Chauhan, felt both pity and frustration toward Arvind. "This man was once a genius.

Now he doesn't even recognise himself in the mirror." They tried different treatments, medications, therapy, even electroshock but nothing brought Arvind back to reality. One day a young intern asked, "Who is he ?" Dr. Chauhan shook his head. "He is beyond saving now."

As time passed, Arvind spoke less and less. He stopped writing equations. He stopped talking to invisible people. He stopped fearing his captors.

One night a nurse found him sitting cross legged on the floor staring at the ceiling, completely still. "Arvind?" she called, but there was no response. She gently touched his shoulder. Finally, he whispered, "I have understood everything. Nothing matters anymore." From that day on, he stopped reacting to the outside world altogether.

He no longer ate unless someone fed him. He didn't respond when spoken to. He barely even blinked. It was as if his soul had left his body, leaving only an empty shell behind.

Arvind Rangnathan, once a brilliant physicist was now a man completely disconnected from the world. He was not dead but he was no longer truly alive.

One day, a Krishna Bhakti yogi named Swami Sampoornanand from ISKCON, New Bombay arrived at the mental asylum. He had been travelling across India, teaching the *Bhagavad Gita* and Yoga to people suffering from mental illness, depression and trauma. The hospital administration, although sceptical, allowed him to conduct sessions with the patients, hoping that, "If nothing else, at least they will learn to sit quietly for an hour."

Swami gathered all the patients in the main hall. Some were laughing, some were crying and some like Arvind sat silently, lost in another world. The swami began singing a simple *Hare Krishna Kirtan.*

HARE KRISHNA, HARE KRISHNA, KRISHNA,
KRISHNA HARE HARE

Most patients ignored him. But something stirred inside Arvind. As the Swami continued singing, Arvind's fingers began twitching. His breath became heavy. Then as if possessed by a divine force, Arvind suddenly stood up. He lifted his trembling hands and in a clear and steady voice began reciting a Shloka from the *Bhagavad Gita,* which meant, "You have the right to perform your prescribed duties, but you are not entitled to the fruits of your action."

The entire hall fell silent. The Swami stopped chanting and turned to look at Arvind, his eyes wide with astonishment. The doctors stunned, unable to believe what they were seeing.

The man who had been unresponsive for months, was standing, his face glowing, reciting sacred verses.

"Who is the man?" they asked.

Dr. Chauhan, the head psychiatrist immediately ordered a full background check. They searched his medical records. They ran his fingerprints in the police database. They also contacted government agencies. Then after hours of investigation, the truth was revealed.

"Oh my God," one doctor whispered, "this man is Arvind Rangnathan, the nuclear scientist who disappeared months ago."

The news spread like wildfire—startling government officials, alerting intelligence agencies, and leaving everyone stunned by the discovery. Meanwhile, Arvind was still in a trance-like state. For the first time in months, he was smiling. The Swami gently placed a hand on Arvind's shoulder and asked, "Do you know, who are you?"

"I was lost but Krishna has called me back," he murmured.

Arvind looked at him, his eyes filled with both clarity and confusion. Tears filled the Swami's eyes, "Yes, my son, Krishna never abandons his devotees."

To the other mentally ill patients, Arvind was not special. They now either ignored or mocked him. One patient, a schizophrenic man often laughed at him and said, "You think you are a scientist? I am the King of Mars."

Another, an elderly woman suffering from dementia whispered, "Poor boy.... they took your mind, didn't they?"

Arvind just smiled gently.

16

After his miraculous recovery, the Government of India wasted no time in reinstating Dr. Arvind Rangnathan. Recognising his genius and the sensitive nature of his work, they appointed him as an "Officer on Special Duty" in the Ministry of Science and Technology. His primary responsibility was to oversee critical operations at the Bhabha Atomic Research Centre (BARC), Mumbai, the heart of India's Nuclear programme.

While the world celebrated his return, deep inside, Arvind was not the same man he once was. As Arvind stepped into his Delhi office, memories of his abduction, the tortures he endured and the days spent lost in insanity, still haunted him.

He often found himself staring at files without reading them. At times, he would hear voices, not of his captors but of Lord Krishna reminding him to remain detached from material pursuits. At night, he struggled with sleeplessness but waking up drenched in sweat as if the Middle Eastern rogues were still haunting him.

"Have I truly returned or am I still lost?" he often wondered.

Despite his appointment, many in the scientific world were sceptical. Some whispered, "Is he mentally stable enough to handle nuclear operation?"

Others feared in silence — reviewing reports, approving crucial projects and ensuring BARC's safety protocols were stronger than ever.

As OSD, Arvind was not just dealing with scientists, he was now involved in high level security matters, Intelligence briefings and government strategies. The RAW (Indian Intelligence Agency) closely monitored him. "We must ensure; he hasn't been compromised," one senior officer told the Prime Minister's office. To make matters worse, foreign intelligence agencies including CIA, Mossad and even ISI (Pakistan's Spy Agency) kept a close eye on his activities.

The Americans wanted to know if he was still working on nuclear advancements. The Middle Eastern groups that had kidnapped him, wanted to ensure, he wasn't planning a revenge.

Arvind however, ignored the noise. His focus remained on duty but deep inside, he knew, he was walking on thin ice.

Despite resuming his scientific duties, Arvind's heart had changed. His days were filled with nuclear research and policy meeting, but his nights were devoted to the *Bhagavad Gita* and Meditation.

While reviewing nuclear policies, he couldn't stop thinking, "Are we really, advancing humanity or are we walking toward destruction?"

Arvind looked out of the window at the setting Sun and realised that power is neither good nor bad, it depends on the one who wields it.

Just when Arvind thought, he had stabilised his life, an alarming intelligence report landed on his desk.

A Rogue organisation, possibly linked to the same group that had kidnapped him, was trying to steal nuclear secrets from India. This time, they were not just targeting technology, they were targeting him for sure.

One evening, as Arvind was reviewing classified files at his Delhi office, he received an urgent call from RAW.

"Sir, we need you at the South Block Head Quarters immediately. It is about national security."

Arvind's heart sank. At RAW's Head Quarters, senior officials presented him with a disturbing report.

A highly organised group, possibly linked to his Middle Eastern captors, was attempting to infiltrate India's nuclear research programme. They were not targeting facilities directly. Instead, they were hunting for an insider someone who had deep knowledge of India's nuclear strategy. The target was clear, Dr. Arvind Rangnathan.

RAW had intercepted communication from a sleeper cell in India, confirming a plan to either abduct or eliminate him.

Arvind faced an impossible choice: he could either resign from his position, step away from nuclear affairs, and return to a simple spiritual life — avoiding any further threats — or he could use his intellect and knowledge to outsmart his enemies and protect India's nuclear security.

As he sat in silent contemplation, he remembered a verse from the *Bhagavad Gita* that says, *"It's better to perish doing one's duty than to follow another's path full of fear."*

That night Arvind made his decision. He would not run; he would not surrender. He would fight back. Arvind with the help of RAW developed a highly classified strategy.

He would pretend to resign from his post making the enemy believe he was no longer useful. While the world thought, he had stepped back, he would secretly lead a team working on advanced nuclear security measures at an undisclosed location.

RAW would use his resignation to flush out spies and sleeper cells embedded within India's scientific community.

His resignation was announced publicly. His enemies relaxed believing he was no longer a threat. But behind the scenes, Arvind was still working, this time in the shadows.

For months, the world believed that Dr. Arvind Rangnathan had left Science for spirituality, but in reality, he was fighting the greatest battle of his life, a battle of intellect, deception and survival.

17

Arvind had spent months in secrecy, living in the shadows, while working on India's nuclear security strategy. His life had become a delicate balance between science, espionage and spirituality.

But fate had one more surprise for him. One evening, as he walked through Lodhi Garden in Delhi, lost in thought, he heard a familiar voice behind him.

"Arvind?"

His body froze. The voice carried both hesitation and longing, a voice he hadn't heard in years, though his heart wanted that echo. He turned around.

Usha's eyes searched his face, trying to read the man before her. He looked older, wearier and yet deeply calm. His eyes no longer carried the restlessness of ambition but rather the detachment of a man who had seen too much. But, deep in his gaze, she could still see a flicker of the old Arvind.

"You look different," she whispered.

Arvind didn't respond immediately. He had spent years suppressing emotions, hardening himself against pain. But now, standing before the woman he once loved, something inside him melted.

For the first time in years, he felt human again.

They sat on a nearby bench, under the soft glow of the setting Sun. Usha spoke about her life, her only son, her marriage, struggles and victories.

Arvind listened silently absorbing every word. Then she asked one question, he wasn't ready for. "And you, Arvind? Did you find what you were looking for?"

Arvind exhaled slowly.

"I found…everything and yet nothing."

Usha held his gaze, "You were never meant to live in shadows, Arvind. You were meant to shine."

Her words struck something deep inside him.

For so long he had believed that detachment was his destiny. But now sitting beside Usha, he realised — maybe he wasn't meant to be lost forever. Usha was continuously telling him everything of her life so far but Arvind wasn't listening anymore. He was watching her eyes, her smile, the way her hair fell over her face.

"Do you remember how you used to tease me about my bad singing?" Usha suddenly asked, pulling him out of his thoughts and his intentional gaze.

"Of course, how could I forget? You had the voice of a broken harmonium."

Usha gasped in fake outrage and hit his shoulder playfully.

"Excuse me, I wasn't that bad."

Arvind sarcastically corrected himself, fine, you were slightly better than a broken Harmonium.

They got up and started walking slowly through the garden, side by side, like they had done years ago.

The way her hand brushed his, sent electric warmth through him. The way she smiled up at him, made him wonder if life had given him a second chance.

At one point, she turned to him, her voice softer now, "Tell me Arvind, do you ever feel lonely?"

All that time there was a silence between them, filled with unspoken emotions, regrets and possibilities but in that fleeting moment, time rebound itself and they were just Arvind and Usha.

After the encounter, Arvind couldn't focus. The scientist in him wanted to continue his mission. The spiritualist in him wanted to walk away from the world. And the human in him longed for something, he thought he had buried long ago.

After his unexpected reunion with Usha, he was negotiating with the warmth of her hand in his. Life, indeed was offering him a second chance, the reality hit him hard like a storm.

The very next day, Arvind forced himself back into his old disciplined life. He buried himself in work, reviewing nuclear security reports, attending closed-door meetings, pretending nothing had changed.

For the first time, the silence in his life felt deafening. He ignored Usha's calls and messages. He avoided places where he might accidentally run into her. He convinced himself that whatever happened was a mistake — a weakness.

But late at night, alone in his Delhi apartment, he found himself staring at the ceiling restless. *Why did her smile keep flashing in his mind? Why did he feel like he had lost something precious all over again?*

Days turned into weeks. Usha eventually stopped calling. She understood what Arvind had chosen. She knew that his world – one of the nuclear secrets, espionage and spiritual detachment had no place for her.

SHE LET HIM GO.

18

Despite his internal turmoil and the deep void left after walking away from Usha, Arvind found solace in his work.

He had always believed in the power of nuclear energy for peace. But he also knew that in a world driven by geopolitical conflicts, India had to be prepared for the worst. That is when he took on his most critical mission yet — guiding Dr. M V. Char, one of the brightest minds at BARC (Babha Atomic Research Centre). Together, they worked on a series of classified nuclear equations that would serve dual purpose — peace and defence.

For peace, they could revolutionise nuclear energy, providing sustainable power across the country and securing India's energy future. For defence, in extreme circumstances, they had the potential to be weaponised beyond any existing nuclear doctrine—ensuring India's absolute sovereignty against any threat.

After months of tireless research, they developed a unique matrix — a set of equations that could extract maximum energy efficiency from nuclear reactions, minimise waste, and use low-enriched uranium for peaceful purposes, while retaining the ability to rapidly transition to high-yield capability if national security was at stake.

The matrix had two defining strengths: first, it could enhance thermal neutron efficiency, making India's next-generation reactors self-sustaining; and second, it remained cleverly concealed within normal energy research — known only to a select few within India's scientific and defence circles who truly understood its strategic potential.

Arvind had done it.

India now possessed a nuclear formula that no foreign intelligence agency could decipher. This was his legacy, but it was also his greatest burden.

As much as Arvind was proud of this breakthrough, a deep moral conflict started brewing within him.

Had he just created a weapon too powerful for mankind to control? Would the political leadership handle it responsibly or would it fall into the wrong hands? Was he truly working for peace or had he just escalated the global arms race?

Late at night in his Delhi apartment, he stared at his reflection in the mirror. For all his detachment from the world and all his spiritual knowledge, he wasn't at peace. He thought of Usha.

Had he made the right choice, abandoning human love for a cause greater than himself? Or had he sacrificed too much?

Even after securing India's nuclear future, Arvind felt empty. He had given his mind to science but had lost his soul in the process. Was there still time to reclaim what he had lost? Or had he gone too far down the path of isolation?

Arvind's life now was a fusion of his expertise in nuclear physics and his spiritual inclinations.

19

Arvind's mind was a battlefield where science, spirituality and love clashed violently. His devotion to nuclear physics was unshakable, yet his spiritual beliefs made him question the very foundations of his research. The equations and theories that once gave him joy, now seemed like dangerous weapons in the wrong hands.

Usha, his only solace, could sense his turmoil but remained helpless. She had always admired his intellect but now she feared it was leading him to destruction. Arvind's concerns were not unfounded, his research had the potential to change the world but also to destroy it. The more he thought about it, the more he felt like a pawn in a game played by powerful politicians who saw his discoveries as mere tools for dominance.

His mind spiralled into conflicts, was he a scientist, a devotee or just a man trapped in forces beyond his control?

He had once believed that knowledge was enlightenment, but now it felt like a curse. Each night, he found himself staring at the *Bhagavad Gita,* searching for answers. "Should I walk away? Or should I fight for what is right?"

Usha's world had shattered the day she lost her husband. The man who had been her anchor, her companion and the father of her young son was gone in an instant — leaving behind memories and an unbearable void. She had no time to grieve properly. Life demanded that she be strong for her child, but deep inside, loneliness gnawed at her soul.

Arvind, already burdened with his own existential crisis, found himself unable to console her. He saw her pain, but he had no answers, no solutions. His own mind was in turmoil, torn between the demands of nuclear physics, the fear of its consequences and the spiritual refuge, he sought in the *Bhagavad Gita.*

Usha's loneliness and Arvind's inner conflict fed into each other, creating a silent storm between them. She needed support, but Arvind was slipping away into his devotion, seeking Krishna's guidance to free him from his miseries. He prayed not for answers but for the release from the moral dilemmas of his research and from the sufferings he saw in Usha's eyes.

20

Arvind found himself in a heated discussion with a group of scientists who dismissed his idea that nuclear physics and spirituality could coexist. To them science was about measurable, testable phenomena, while spirituality belonged to the realm of faith and subjective experience. One of the Physicist, Dr. E.S.S. Menon challenged him, "Arvind, science is based on empirical evidence, whereas spirituality is based on belief. How can you claim they are connected?"

Arvind remained calm and replied, "Let me start with Hindu mythology. Hanuman's childhood tale of leaping toward the Sun holds a fascinating parallel regarding the Sun's distance from Earth. The verse *'Yug Sahastra Yojana Bhanu'* is often interpreted as follows:

- 1 Yug = 12,000 years
- 1 Sahastra = 1,000
- 1 Yojana = 8 miles

When multiplied, this gives a distance that's remarkably close to the modern scientific estimate of the Sun's distance from Earth.

"Therefore 12000 × 1000 × 8 = 96 million miles
which is equal to 96M × 1.6 =153.6million kilometres.

"As per scientific calculations, the average distance between Sun and Earth is approximately 149.6 million kilometres. This suggests that ancient sages had advanced astronomical knowledge."

Arvind further explained how quantum mechanics challenges our classical understanding of reality.

"In quantum physics, particles exist in multiple states until observed — a phenomenon known as wave-particle duality.

"Doesn't this resemble how quantum physics shows that reality changes depending on observations?"

Another scientist, Dr. Udesh Sharma asked, "But where does spirituality fit into nuclear reactions?"

Arvind smiled and quoted Einstein's equation, "$E=mc^2$, matter and energy are interchangeable.

"The *Bhagavad Gita* states that the soul (ATMA) is eternal and cannot be destroyed. The soul is neither burned by fire nor cut by weapons.

"Similarly, in physics, energy cannot be created or destroyed, only transformed. If modern physics accepts that energy is eternal, why is it so hard to accept that consciousness might also be eternal?"

Another scientist Dr.Unnikrishnan interrupted, "Nuclear energy is a force of destruction, not spirituality."

Arvind countered, "It depends on how it's used. Just like Shiva, the cosmic force of destruction, paves the way for creation, likewise nuclear reactions can either destroy cities or power them with energy."

He reminded them that Robert Oppenheimer, the father of the atomic bomb, himself quoted the *Bhagavad Gita* when he saw the first nuclear explosion. He also quoted that the mind is the best friend of one who has conquered it but for one who has failed to do so, it remains the greatest enemy.

The room fell silent. The scientists, though not fully convinced, were forced to acknowledge that Arvind's perspective was not irrational. It was simply a different way of looking at the universe.

Dr. E.S.S. Menon finally spoke, "Maybe we were too quick to dismiss your ideas. Perhaps science and spirituality are not so different after all."

Arvind smiled. He knew, he had planted a seed of thought. Whether they accepted it or not, the journey of integrating science and spirituality had begun.

21

Arvind's mind was again a battlefield. His research in nuclear physics had once been his life's purpose, a pursuit of knowledge that could revolutionise energy, medicine and technology. But now, all he could see was its destructive potential. The deeper he went into his work, the more restless he became. The equations on his blackboard no longer looked like symbols of progress, they felt like warnings of impending doom.

He had read about Hiroshima and Nagasaki, how a single bomb had wiped out cities in an instant, reducing thousands of innocent lives to mere shadows on walls. He imagined the horror of such a catastrophe in the modern world, where nuclear stockpiles had multiplied beyond comprehension.

One evening after hours of unsuccessful attempts to focus, he stood before the *Bhagavad Gita*, seeking solace. He remembered Krishna's words to Arjun, *"The one who works for the welfare of all beings attains liberation."* Arvind thought, if science did not serve humanity, then what was its purpose? Was his loyalty to his research, his nation — or the survival of the entire human race?

Then the words of his colleague, Dr.Menon echoed and rang in his mind, "Arvind you are a scientist first, nations compete, but scientific progress must continue."

Arvind remembered his response, "Science without ethics is a curse. If nuclear physics falls into the wrong hands, it will not be a nation that suffers, it will be all of humanity."

Unable to contain his emotions, Arvind just collapsed before the *Bhagavad Gita* and pleaded, "Krishna, give me a sign. Should I continue this work, knowing it might lead to disaster? Or should I walk away?"

He remembered Oppenheimer, who had quoted the *Gita* upon witnessing the first nuclear explosion. *Now I have become death, the destroyer of worlds.*

A sudden realisation struck him. It wasn't Arvind's duty to just create but to ensure that his knowledge was never used for destruction. His restlessness began to ease, but the path ahead was still unclear. All he knew was that his duty lay beyond patriotism, his duty was to humanity itself.

The next morning, Arvind attended a high-level meeting at the research facility. Senior scientists and government officials were discussing advancements in nuclear technology focusing on its "strategic military applications". As the discussions continued, Arvind stood up abruptly and shouted, "I cannot remain silent anymore."

The room fell silent, Dr. Menon, Dr. Sharma and senior Government officials frowned, "Arvind, what are you doing?"

Arvind voice was firm, "We claim to be advancing science for the future, but are we even thinking about the consequences? If we continue down this path, we are inviting global destruction. Have we forgotten Hiroshima and Nagasaki?"

One of the guys smirked, "That's not our concern, Dr. Arvind. We are scientists, let the policymakers decide how to use our research."

Arvind lost his cool but very politely with determination said, "No, we are not just scientists, we are human beings as well first, if we create something capable of mass destruction, we are equally responsible for its consequences."

His words did not sit well with many. Over the next few days, he noticed strange behaviour among his colleagues. Some avoided him, some whispered behind his back.

One evening, Dr. Udesh Sharma visited him. "Arvind, we respect your views, but you are making powerful enemies. You should step back before it's too late."

Arvind smiled sadly and said, "Dr. Sharma, what is the purpose of knowledge if it serves destruction? I cannot step back now."

Soon he received an indirect warning – a letter with a single sentence in bold.

Patriotism is above personal beliefs,
do not interfere.

It was clear, he was being watched.

22

Usha had been silently observing the storm gathering around Arvind. The whispers of betrayal, the threats disguised as warnings and the looming danger of exile, all of it worried her deeply. She knew Arvind was strong but even the strongest warriors could falter when faced with isolation and relentless opposition.

One evening, she called him and asked, "Arvind, can we meet?"

Arvind exhausted from the days of battles, sighed, "Usha, this is not the right time."

"It is," she insisted, "more than ever."

They met in a quiet park, away from the prying eyes of officials. Arvind looked drained, his eyes carried the weight of the world, but his resolve remained unshaken.

Usha placed a hand on his shoulder and gently said, "I know what you are going through. I know the warnings, the threats, the isolation. And I know your dilemma."

Arvind exhaled, "Usha, I am not afraid for myself, but they will go to any extent to silence me."

"Arvind, you always told me that duty to humanity is greater than duty to a nation. If that is true, then you cannot step back now."

Arvind looked at her surprised, "You think I should continue?"

Usha smiled, "You are not just fighting for yourself, you are fighting for a future where science serves peace, not destruction. If you stop now, what message will you leave for the next generation?"

Arvind fell silent. He had expected her to ask him to be careful, to reconsider his instance. But instead, she was strengthening his will and supporting him.

"I lost my husband to fate," Usha continued, her voice steady. "But I will not lose you to fear. Whatever happens, Arvind, I will stand by you."

Arvind felt an unfamiliar warmth in his chest. He was not alone. For the first time in weeks, he smiled.

"Thank you, Usha. This battle has just become easier."

Usha's words reignited his purpose. Warnings could threaten him but they would not break him. Now, he was ready to face whatever came next, not as a lone scientist but as a man with a mission, and with someone who believed in him completely.

23

As the pressure mounted, Arvind faced a defining choice. The first option was to resign and escape — a safer route, but one that meant abandoning his responsibility. The second was to stay and resist — a far more dangerous path, yet one that aligned with his deepest sense of moral duty.

That night again he sat before the *Bhagavad Gita,* searching for answers. His eyes fell upon Krishna's words to Arjun which meant that, you have a right to perform your duty, but never to the fruits of your actions. The answer was clear. His duty was not to protect himself but to ensure his knowledge was used for good.

Instead of resigning, Arvind devised a bold plan — a secret mission to protect knowledge from destruction and misuse. He began encrypting and compartmentalising his research, ensuring that no single entity could fully weaponise it.

He reached out to scientists in other countries who shared his concerns, forming a covert coalition committed to keeping nuclear research peaceful. At the same time, he started publishing papers that highlighted the moral responsibilities of scientists, subtly warning the global community against reckless nuclear proliferation.

Though he knew, he was making enemies, he also knew, he was fulfilling his true dharma, protecting humanity, not just saving a nation.

As Arvind stood before his lab window, staring at the night sky, he whispered, "Krishna, I do not know where this path will lead. But I will follow it, even if I stand alone."

His battle had begun. Not a battle of weapons, but a battle of conscience, ethics and humanity itself. Now, the consequences of his rebellion began unfolding before him.

A week after his speech against militarisation, subtle but powerful attacks began. His funding requests were denied without explanation. His research team was assigned to other projects isolating him. He was accused of leaking classified information, though he had done nothing of the sort.

One evening, Dr. Udesh Sharma again met him in private.

"Arvind, they are coming for you. The government believes you are a threat to national security. Then be prepared for what follows."

A few days later, Arvind was summoned to meet a high ranking official, Ajit Jogi, a man known from NSA (National Security Advisor) for handling "difficult" scientists.

The official leaned back and forward, then finally spoke, "Dr. Arvind Rangnathan, you are a brilliant scientist, we don't want to lose you. But your recent actions are concerning us rather bothering us."

Arvind remained silent.

The man continued "We can offer you a way out a prestigious international project with unlimited resources and protection. But you must stop interfering in national matters. No more anti-nuclear talks, no more disruptions."

Arvind knew, this was a temptation, a bribe disguised as an opportunity. He smiled faintly, "I appreciate the offer, but my conscience is not for sale."

Ajit Jogi's expression hardened, "Very well, now that you have made your decision. Be ready."

A scientist was turned as an enemy of the state. The government had labelled Arvind, a traitor, a threat to national security and a dangerous dissenter. His refusal to comply with their demands had sealed his fate. But instead of exile or house arrest, they decided to make an example of him.

It was 2.30 am when the knock came. Not a polite knock but an aggressive pounding. Before Arvind could react, his door was kicked open. Five armed officers stormed in, grabbing him before he could even process what was happening.

"Dr. Arvind, you are under arrest for espionage, conspiracy against the state and anti-national activities."

No explanation, no trial — just brute force. As they dragged him away, his neighbours peeked through their windows, whispering in fear. The once respected scientist was now a prisoner of the state.

Arvind was thrown into a secret underground facility, a place where prisoners had no names, only numbers.

For weeks, he was subjected to brutal interrogations. He had sleep deprivation due to bright lights burning in his cell 24/7. He got regular beatings, not to kill him, but to break his strong determination. There was psychological warfare — recordings of people calling him a traitor, fake news declaring his betrayal, and constant threats to Usha and anyone close to him.

The officials wanted one thing — A CONFESSION. They needed him to admit he was a spy, to justify their actions to the public.

But Arvind did not break. Every night, he repeated to himself, *SATYAMEVA JAYATE – TRUTH ALONE TRIUMPHS.*

After months of torture, the government decided to put him on trial, not to seek justice but to destroy his reputation. The courtroom was rigged from the start. The

Judge was handpicked. The evidence was fabricated. The media had already labelled him a villain.

As he stood in the courtroom, weak but unbroken, the prosecutor sneered, "Dr Arvind, you betrayed your country. What do you have to say for yourself."

Arvind looked straight ahead and spoke clearly, "I have betrayed no one. I have only spoken the truth. You fear me not because I am guilty, but because I refused to be silent."

The judge banged the gavel, "Silence the accused. He is guilty of treason."

The government never wanted to execute him. They wanted him to suffer. His sentence: life imprisonment in a high-security labour camp, the complete erasure of his research from history, and his name blacklisted from all scientific records — as if he had never existed.

As he was dragged out of the courtroom, Usha screamed his name but the guards held her back.

For the first time, Arvind felt fear, not for himself, but for those who still believed in him.

The labour camp was a hellhole. Days were spent breaking rocks under the scorching Sun. Nights were spent in a freezing cell alone. He was given rotten food, barely enough to survive.

Every day, the guards taunted him, "Was it worth it scientist?"

Yet he refused to bow.

At night in his mind, he recited the *Bhagavad Gita* and thought about Krishna. Even in suffering, there was purpose. Even in darkness, there was light.

Outside Usha was not silent. She had spent years gathering evidence, rallying international support, secretly contacting human rights organisations.

24

The entire nuclear world became obsessed with Arvind's knowledge of nuclear physics, eager to draw him into their establishments — by any means necessary, right or wrong, fair or unfair — especially the rogue elements. It seems like Arvind has reached a level of genius and influence where the world sees him a crucial asset, perhaps due to his ground breaking work in nuclear physics or his deep spiritual insights. Governments, intelligence agencies, corporate giants and even religious institutions were vying to have him on their side, willing to use any means necessary, be it persuasion, coercion or deception to win his allegiance.

All along Arvind, true to his spiritual values was rejecting temptations of power and wealth.

The world due to Arvind's stand had largely forgotten him. His name had been erased from scientific circles and even the Government of India had buried his existence deep within a high security labour camp. But not everyone had moved on. A rogue international group known for smuggling high-profile political prisoners out of captivity, had taken interest in his case.

The rogues were a mix of disillusioned ex-intelligence officers, mercenaries, underground activists who believed that Arvind was more than just a prisoner, he was a symbol of resistance against scientific oppression.

Their leader, an ex-CIA operative named Col. Simoes, had only one goal — extract Arvind without a trace.

Their plan was dangerous: disrupt the camp's security system, set off explosions near the watchtowers to create a diversion, and smuggle Arvind out using stolen military transport. Every step was a gamble, but it was the only chance they had.

It was past midnight when the first explosion went off near the camp's perimeter. The guards panicked, thinking it was an external attack. At the same time, two of Col. Simoes' men disguised as prison officers, entered Arvind's barrack.

"Dr. Arvind Rangnathan, we are getting you out of here, now."

Arvind, weak from years of hard labour, struggled to stand and asked, "Who sent you?"

"That's none of your business," said one of the two intruders.

With the sirens blaring and search lights sweeping the camp, Arvind was rushed towards an armoured vehicle stolen from the Government's own convoy. Just as they were about to drive through the main gate, a roadblock appeared.

The guards opened fire. Bullets ripped through the night as the rogues fired back, Col. Simoes threw a smoke grenade, clouding their vision. With one final push, they rammed through the barrier but the rogue group had underestimated the Indian security forces. They had expected a clean escape, but the government had been tracking them all along.

As their armoured vehicle sped through the dark wilderness, drones from the Indian military locked onto their position. Within minutes, helicopters and ground forces surrounded them. The night sky was filled with the thunder of chopper blades and the glare of flood lights.

A voice boomed through the loud speaker.

DROP YOUR WEAPONS, YOU ARE SURROUNDED.

Col. Simoes gritted his teeth, "No way we are surrendering."

The rogues, heavily armed, fought back fiercely. The Indian forces, determined to eliminate them, launched a relentless assault. Bullets flew in all directions, explosions shook the ground, and screams echoed through the night.

Col. Simoes tried to drag Arvind toward an escape route, but a sniper's bullet ripped through his skull, dropping him instantly. One by one, the rogues fell. Their escape mission had turned into a blood-bath.

The commander of the Indian forces approached Arvind with a gun pointed at him.

"Dr. Arvind, do you understand what you have done?"

"Don't you realise that your attitude towards your nation had done such a crime. Do you have any explanation?"

Arvind in a steady voice replied, "I did what my conscience told me, if truth is a crime, then I am guilty."

There was long silence. The commander gave a nod and two soldiers grabbed Arvind, pinning his wrists.

He was not free, but he was alive.

25

Instead of sending Arvind back to labour camp, the government decided to handle him differently.

A secret tribunal was constituted to decide his fate — far from public eyes. He would be placed under solitary confinement, with no access to books, science, or even the *Bhagavad Gita.* His knowledge would be exploited for military research, whether he agreed or not.

He had escaped death, but at what cost?

Arvind was silenced, locked away in an unknown facility, his fate uncertain, but Usha refused to accept defeat.

She knew that if she didn't act, Arvind would either die in captivity or be forced to build weapons instead of peace-driven nuclear energy.

Usha reached out to renowned nuclear physicists, human rights activists and global organisations that supported the ethical use of nuclear science.

She began by reaching out to global institutions. She contacted the International Atomic Energy Agency (IAEA) to prove that Arvind's work was intended for peaceful purposes. She appealed to the United Nations Human Rights Council (UNHRC) to expose the wrongful imprisonment of a scientist. Finally, she reached out to Western universities and research institutes, rallying scientists to speak out against the injustice.

Letters, petitions and research papers flooded global platforms, demanding Arvind's release. Usha also knew that public pressure was more powerful than secret diplomacy. She contacted international journalists and whistleblower groups.

Usha's efforts paid and articles appeared in *The New York Times, The Guardian,* and *Al Jazeera,* calling Arvind a prisoner of conscience.

Social media campaigns with "FREE ARVIND" started trending. A leaked video of Arvind's prison conditions sparked global outrage.

Within weeks, diplomats and human rights group started questioning the Indian government. The growing pressure forced several global leaders to intervene.

The European Union issued a formal statement demanding a fair trial for Arvind. The United States hinted at sanctions if India continued to suppress scientific freedom. The IAEA threatened to revoke India's participation in peaceful nuclear programme unless Arvind was freed.

Now the Indian government was in a dilemma. If they released Arvind, they risked exposing their internal political struggles. If they kept him imprisoned, they faced severe diplomatic backlash.

In a bold move, Usha delivered a powerful speech at an international summit on nuclear ethics. With tears in her eyes but fire in her voice, she said, "Arvind dedicated his life to science, to humanity. He never sought war, only peace. Is this how we treat the minds who dream of a better world?"

Her words shook the nation. Public protests erupted in India, forcing the government to reconsider. Under immense global pressure, the Indian government finally agreed to a conditional release: Arvind would be freed, but he must not leave India. He could continue his research but under strict government supervision. Any further contact with foreign agencies could lead to his re-arrest.

When the government offered him a conditional release, Arvind firmly refused.

"I will not compromise my principles. If I am to be free, it will be on my own terms not as a pawn in anyone's game."

The pressure on the authorities had become unbearable. International organisations continued to issue warnings of sanctions and diplomatic fallout. Mass protests erupted across India, with students, scientists, and activists demanding Arvind's unconditional release. Finally, the Supreme Court was petitioned to review his case, forcing the judiciary to intervene.

The government could no longer justify his retention. They had to save face without appearing weak.

26

On a cold morning after years of confinement, Arvind was finally released. There were no conditions, no restrictions. As he walked out of the captivity, Usha was waiting for him.

Tears welled up in her eyes as she whispered, "You did it, Arvind. The world stood with you."

But Arvind ever the realist, replied, "The fight is not over, Usha, now we must ensure nuclear energy serves humanity not destruction."

Realising they could no longer control Arvind; the government appointed another scientist who would toe their line and align nuclear research with military interests. The new scientist Dr. Vinod Batra was brilliant but lacked Arvind's moral compass.

He began agreeing to government policies without question. He prioritised defence applications over peaceful energy research. In public, he dismissed Arvind's ideals, calling them "idealistic and outdated."

27

Arvind knew the real battle had only just begun. He had to counter government propaganda that had twisted nuclear science for military gain. He had to rebuild his reputation and research facilities after years of imprisonment. Most importantly, he had to convince the scientific community that nuclear energy must be a tool for peace — not destruction. With Usha by his side, he formed an independent research Institute, free from political influence.

Years had passed, and Usha's son, Mukund, had now graduated with a degree in nuclear physics. He had inherited his mother's resilience and Arvind's passion for ethical science. When Mukund returned home with his degree, Usha introduced him to Arvind.

"Mukund, you have the opportunity to work under one of the greatest minds of our time. I want you to follow Arvind's principle — science for humanity, not for destruction. Arvind, now a seasoned fighter for nuclear peace saw hope in the young man's eyes. Taking Mukund under his wing, Arvind began shaping him into a scientist with the integrity.

He taught him the secrets of nuclear energy not just as a scientist but as a responsibility. He shared the struggles of his past, warning against the temptations of power and the political influence. He trained him to question authority, to challenge decisions that could lead to destruction.

"Knowledge is a weapon, Mukund," Arvind told him. "But you must decide whether to use it to protect or destroy."

As Mukund gained recognition, the Government of India took notice. They knew, he was Arvind's protégé and they wanted to recruit him to counter Arvind's influence.

Officials offered Mukund a lucrative job, promising wealth and recognition if he worked for them. Dr.Vinod Batra tried to lure him, saying, "Your ideas will shape the future. Don't waste time with outdated ideals."

They pressured Usha, warning her that Arvind's path could ruin Mukund's career. But Usha stood firm.

"My son will walk the path of truth. He will not be another pawn in your game." And Mukund inspired by Arvind's journey, refused all offers.

"I choose knowledge for peace. I choose Arvind's vision."

With Mukund now part of his mission, Arvind saw a future where his ideals would not die.

But the challenges were far from over. Would the government attempt to sabotage Arvind's institute?

Could Mukund withstand the pressure, or would he be tempted by power? And would Dr. Vinod Batra become their greatest adversary?

As Arvind, Usha and Mukund stood together, they knew one thing, this was just the beginning of the next great battle. Arvind knew that government would never stop in its attempts to control Mukund. They had already ruined his life once; he wouldn't let them do the same to Usha's son. Determined to shield Mukund from threats, manipulations and political traps, Arvind made a bold decision.

Using his international influence, Arvind arranged for Mukund to study in the United States, where he would be under the direct supervision of the International Atomic Energy Agency (IAEA).

It was a strategic move. The IAEA would ensure that Mukund's research was used solely for peaceful purposes. He would be safe from political interference in India, and he could access cutting-edge nuclear technology in a free and ethical environment.

When Arvind told Usha about the plan, she was both proud and fearful.

"Arvind, sending him away means losing him but keeping him here means risking everything."

Arvind held her hands firmly and said softly, "Usha we have suffered enough. Mukund must live the life we couldn't."

28

When Arvind and Usha told Mukund about the opportunity to study in the U.S., he listened carefully. Then he looked at both of them and firmly put forward his condition.

"I will go, but only if you both stay together and look after each other."

Arvind and Usha were shocked by his words.

"Mukund, what are you saying?" Usha asked. "We are not a couple. We are not even married."

Arvind added, "Mukund our relationship is not like that, we are bound by respect, friendship and a shared mission, nothing more."

But Mukund smiled knowingly and replied, "Even Radha and Krishna were not married, yet their bond was eternal and divine. You both are spiritually connected to them. Who else but you two can understand such a sacred relationship."

His concluding statement was, "There is something called 'platonic love'."

His words stunned them both into silence. Arvind lowered his gaze, lost in thought. Was Mukund right? Had he grown so mature, so confident, to express himself with such authority? Had he and Usha truly become inseparable — in purpose and in soul?

Usha's eyes moistened. She had never thought of it this way, but deep down, she knew: she and Arvind had become each other's greatest support, despite all their struggles.

Mukund continued, gently but firmly, "Maa, Sir ji, life is uncertain. I cannot leave you peacefully if I know you are both alone. You need each other more than you admit."

Arvind finally spoke, his voice filled with emotions, "Mukund, I have always followed Krishna's teachings. But today, you reminded me of something I had forgotten. Radha and Krishna's love was never about rituals, but about divine connection. Maybe, maybe you are right."

Usha wiped her tears and said softly, "I always saw Arvind as my guiding force, but I never acknowledged how much I needed him, not just as a mentor, but as a part of my life."

They both looked at each other and for the first time, they truly accepted their bond. It was not bound by society, marriage or labels. It was something deeper and purer.

Finally, Arvind and Usha turned to Mukund and said in unison.

"We promise, we will stay together and look after each other."

Arvind smiled in satisfaction. The sacred bond of Radha and Krishna found a reflection in Arvind and Usha's companionship.

The night before Mukund's flight, Arvind and Usha sat with him. Mukund looked up to Arvind and said, "I don't want to leave you in this battle alone."

Arvind smiled and placed a reassuring hand on his shoulder.

"Sometimes, the greatest warriors fight from far. Your mission is bigger than me, bigger than us. Go, learn and when the time is right—return."

At the airport, Usha hugged Mukund tightly.

"Stay true to the path Arvind has shown you, *beta.* The world will test you, but never forget why you chose this path."

Arvind also sent him a text message.

Satyamev Jayate.

Karmanye vadhikaraste ma phaleshu kadachana.

(You have the right to perform your actions, but not to the fruits of those actions.)

29

As Arvind turned away from the airport he whispered a silent prayer to Lord Krishna.

Protect him my lord. Let him succeed where I could not.

Now, Arvind stood alone against a system that saw him as a threat. As he walked, thoughts swirled in his mind: Would Mukund's research in the U.S. help bring nuclear peace to the world? Would he one day return to complete the mission I could not finish?

Usha was silent and sad throughout their return from the airport. Arvind had always been a fighter against ignorance, against corruption, against the misuse of nuclear science but he now stood alone.

Mukund was gone pursuing his mission in the U.S. Usha had fulfilled her role, ensuring Mukund's safe passage.

The government still watched Arvind closely, waiting for a chance to break him. He was mentally exhausted, his body growing weaker with age but his spirit remained unshaken.

Arvind often spent his nights alone, lost in thought. Had he done enough? Was Mukund truly safe from the same forces that had once tried to silence him? Would his dream of nuclear peace survive without him? And was he taking good care of Usha, as he had promised Mukund?

Usha had no regrets but was constantly bothered about the physical and mental health of Arvind.

The struggle had left him drained but not hopeless. He also knew that his mission was larger than his own lifetime.

One evening, as he sat in meditation with the *Bhagavad Gita* open in front of him, he whispered, "Krishna, I am tired. But I cannot stop. I need your strength."

A verse from Gita echoed again in his mind:

"Karmanye vadhikkarasteMa phaleshu kadachana."
(You have the right to perform your duty, but never to the fruits of your actions.)

Arvind smiled faintly. He had never fought for personal gain, only for truth for humanity.

THIS WAS HIS TRUE VICTORY.

Though physically weaker, Arvind gathered his strength. He continued writing, documenting everything, he had learned so that no one could erase his vision. He mentored young scientists in secret, passing on his wisdom. He worked with human rights groups, ensuring that the global scientific community kept an eye on India's nuclear policies.

He was one man against an entire system, but he refused to surrender because hope was still alive. As long as he breathed, he would keep fighting.

30

In the United States, Mukund was excelling in his research on nuclear energy for peace. His work was being recognised globally and he was quickly becoming a respected scientist.

But amidst the equations and experiments, Mukund felt something missing. A question often troubled him.

Science can harness immense power, but what guides its purpose? Where does true wisdom come from?

His search led him to a place of unexpected answers – ISKCON (International Society for Krishna Consciousness). At ISKCON, Mukund met devotees, scholars and monks who spoke about the *Bhagavad Gita's* wisdom in ways he had never imagined.

One evening, during a discourse, a monk said, "Just as an atom contains unimaginable energy, the soul contains infinite potential, true science and true spirituality are not separate. They are two sides of the same truth."

Mukund felt a deep connection to these words. He realised that Arvind had been right all along — nuclear physics and spirituality were not opposites but complimentary forces.

Just as the Sun fuels all life, nuclear energy could either destroy or uplift humanity, depending on the intent behind it.

From that day on, Mukund became a regular visitor to ISKCON. He meditated on Krishna's teachings, understanding how morality must guide science. He applied spiritual wisdom to his research ensuring that nuclear technology was used only for the welfare of humanity.

He dedicated himself to Arvind's vision but with a renewed sense of purpose, one that blended both scientific logic and spiritual ethics.

One day, after an intense spiritual session at ISKCON, Mukund wrote an emotional letter to Arvind and Usha.

> *Sir, Maa, I now understand what you both have been fighting for. Science without wisdom is dangerous. But when guided by Krishna's eternal truth, it can become a force for peace. I promise to uphold this vision. The world will not misuse our knowledge, not while I am here.*

As Arvind read the letter, a tear rolled down his cheek.

"Krishna has chosen him," he whispered.

Usha smiled proudly yet emotionally. Mukund had not only continued Arvind's legacy but he had elevated it to a divine mission.

31

The government was determined that nuclear power was not just for humanity but also for national security. They wanted Arvind to obey, to develop advanced nuclear weapons under the pretext of deterrence, but Arvind resisted.

"We already have enough ourselves. Why create more destruction?"

The politicians and military leaders saw him as an obstacle to their ambitions. They again started torturing him and Usha directly or indirectly. For months, Arvind had suffered illegal detention and inhuman torture.

The world was watching.

Across major cities, massive demonstrations erupted. University students marched with banners.

Science is for peace, not for oppression.

Scientists resigned from government projects in protest of Arvind's torture. Human rights activists filed petitions in International Courts. International pressure was mounting. Youth had turned against them.

The relentless protests and international pressure not only eased Arvind's obstacles but toppled the existing government and six months later, a new progressive leadership took charge committed to global peace and scientific integrity.

Despite all the torture and betrayal, Arvind did not seek revenge. Instead, he chose to lead with wisdom.

The new government appointed him as Head of the Nuclear Policy Council, giving him full authority to ensure that nuclear technology was used solely for peaceful purposes. He began collaborating with international scientists and regulatory bodies such as the IAEA, working to prevent nuclear disasters. He focused on strengthening nuclear protocols and ensuring that the technology could not be misused by any political or military entity.

Arvind was accepted as a guardian of humanity. Arvind's first move was to rewrite the nation's nuclear doctrine. He declared:

The power of the atom must never be a tool of destruction but a force for progress. Nuclear energy belongs to humanity not war.

Under his leadership, several key changes were introduced. There was a total ban on nuclear weapons testing and development. The focus shifted towards using nuclear energy for sustainable development, including clean energy production, medical research, and agricultural innovation.

His policies were hailed globally and many nations followed his model. He also advised Mukund working in the U.S. to ensure that the next generations carried forward this mission.

Arvind, once persecuted scientist was now world's leading nuclear policy architect and as he stood before the United Nations addressing the world leaders, he quoted the *Bhagavad Gita*:

> *Whenever there is a decline in righteousness and increase in injustice, I manifest myself to restore balance.*

He looked at the assembled world leaders, scientists and human rights activists and then with a calm yet commanding voice, he spoke.

"No nation shall develop nuclear weapons beyond self-defence limits.

"Nuclear technology must be used exclusively for energy, medicine and human welfare.

"An independent international body will monitor nuclear programmes worldwide."

32

While Arvind had redefined nuclear policy, it was Mukund who changed nuclear physics itself.

Working tirelessly in the United States under the direct supervision of the IAEA, he pursued a vision far beyond any scientist's imagination. It was his dream to develop a mathematical equation that would ensure nuclear energy could only be used for peaceful purposes and never for destruction.

After years of research, Mukund made a historic breakthrough. He discovered a set of equations that fundamentally altered nuclear reactions.

His equations enabled nuclear energy to be harnessed for electricity, medicine and agriculture. However, they made it impossible to weaponise the same energy for bombs or military use.

Any attempt to modify the equation for destruction would automatically cause a catastrophic chain reaction.

This was Mukund's holy approach of nuclear physics — a discovery that forever ended the threat of nuclear war.

When Mukund presented his findings to the IAEA and top nuclear scientists, the world was shocked and awed.

His equations were tested and validated globally. For the first time in history, nuclear energy had a built-in safeguard against war. Nation that once hoarded nuclear weapons now had to rethink their strategies.

The United Nations declared his discovery as the "Greatest Scientific Contribution to World Peace."

Mukund was nominated for the Nobel Prize in Physics and his name was etched in the history as the man who disarmed the atom. After the successful completion of his ground breaking mission, Mukund prepared to leave the United States.

His final days in the country were filled with scientific conference in his honour, where leading physicists praised his revolutionary work.

A farewell ceremony was organised by the IAEA, recognising his unparalleled contribution in ensuring nuclear energy remained a tool for peace.

Meetings with top global leaders who assured him that his vision would shape the future of nuclear policy.

On the day of departure, the airport was crowded with students, fellow scientists and well-wishers. As he boarded the flight back to India, the Director of the IAEA shook his hand and said, "You did what no one else could. The world will always remember Mukund and Arvind."

As the plane took off, Mukund looked out at the horizon knowing that his real mission was just beginning.

His mentor, Arvind and his mother were waiting for him and so was the next chapter of his journey for humanity. As he stepped off the plane, he saw thousands of people cheering for him.

Arvind now older and frail, had tears in his eyes.

"You have done what I could only dream of, Mukund."

Mukund smiled, bent down and touched Arvind's feet. "I have followed the path, you showed me, Sir."

That evening, standing on the banks of the Yamuna, Mukund looked at the setting sun and said, "Science and spirituality are not separate. Together, they have saved humanity."

33

Back in his home country, Arvind's leadership led to historic transformations. Nuclear research shifted entirely toward clean energy. A new generation of scientists, led by Mukund, carried forward his legacy.

India became the first country to declare nuclear energy as a tool solely for progress, not war. The new government, once sceptical, now saw Arvind as a national hero. Even the common revered him, not as a politician but as a visionary scientist who had sacrificed everything for truth.

After years of struggle, Arvind finally fell at peace. One evening as he sat in ISKCON garden, Usha came with Mukund and sat beside him. She smiled and said, "You did it, Arvind. The world listens to you now."

Usha then placed the *Bhagavad Gita* in his hands and said, "You never fought for power, you only fought for Dharma. Just like Krishna guided Arjun, you guided Mukund, you guided the world."

Tears welled up in Arvind's eyes. He had found his true purpose – not just in nuclear physics, but in the service of humanity.

"Mukund will follow your legacy now."

34

Yes, decay is a fundamental natural phenomenon that applies to everything living or dead in the universe, including Arvind. Arvind despite his deep spiritual connection and scientific brilliance, is not exempted from the natural law of decay, whether it's physical ageing, mental struggles or the eventual decline of his influence in his specialised field.

As Arvind was ageing, his body slightly started failing perhaps due to chronic illness or general frailty. His sharp mind once balancing between spirituality and nuclear physics, had started showing signs of decline. His struggle was between accepting this condition as part of life or wanting to contribute more before it was too late.

Usha throughout was trying to convince him to rest, take care of himself or even reconsider his vigorous intellectual pursuits, but Arvind, being deeply involved in his spiritual and scientific journey was not prioritising his own health.

Usha got on insisting and persisting upon him but things mostly went on deaf ears. She felt helpless, torn between wanting Arvind to fight for his health, but she understood that he had surrendered to the natural process of life. Over the time, Arvind's health gradually worsened, perhaps due to heart disease, partly Parkinson's or simply the frailty of old age.

His hands started trembling and his sharp memory once, began to fade at times. He started struggling to do things, he once did effortlessly, however his mind though occasionally clouded, still retained glimpses of brilliance.

Usha, deeply attached to Arvind, watched him from afar, her heart heavy with pain and helplessness. She did her best for him ensuring, he took his medicines, feeding him when he was refusing to eat and she was constantly sitting by his bedside reading from the *Bhagavad Gita* or discussing physics, hoping to keep his mind engaged. She repeatedly urged him to fight, to take care of himself, but Arvind, though grateful seemed to accept his fate with a quiet surrender.

He reassured her, "Usha, my body is decaying but my soul is only returning to its source. I am not leaving, I am transforming."

Mukund, caught up in fulfilling Arvind's mission, failed to see the urgency of his mentor's condition. He believed, he was honouring Arvind by ensuring his vision lived on. However, as Arvind's condition worsened, Usha confronted Mukund, "What good is a mission if the man who inspired it, is left alone in his final days?"

This moment shook Mukund. Realising his mistake, he rushed back to Arvind, just in time to have one last conversation and a final glimpse of his mentor.

Mukund sat beside Arvind, he apologised. But Arvind, with his fading strength, smiled and placed a weak hand over Mukund's.

"You have done well, Mukund. Science and spirituality are both paths to the same truth. Do not mourn my decay. Let it remind you that even the Universe is in a constant state of transformation. Seek the eternal my child, not the fleeting."

Arvind also recited a verse from the *Bhagavad Gita* which meant, *The soul is neither born nor does it die.*

Usha held his hand, tears falling silently. Mukund too, realised that his moment was not just about loss, but about understanding Arvind's greatest lesson — that life, science and spirituality all pointed to the same ultimate truth.

On the eve of his passing, Arvind walked slowly to the banks of the Yamuna. The river, a witness to history and devotion, mirrored his own life. Once vibrant, now calm, yet endlessly flowing. The setting sun painted the sky in shades of orange and crimson, reflecting the transition between day and night, between life and death. He was sitting still as if he was conversing with the universe itself.

Usha, realising, Arvind had gone for a long time, found him sitting there, lost in thought, unmoving. She called out softly, "Arvind, it's getting late. Let's go home." But Arvind didn't respond immediately.

His lips barely moved as he whispered, "Usha, have you ever noticed how the Sun doesn't fight his setting? It simply let go knowing, it will rise again somewhere else."

Tears rolled in Usha's eyes. She understood.

This is Arvind's farewell. She gently helped him up, supporting his frail body as they walked back home. For the first time, Arvind leaned on her, not just for balance but in trust, in silent acknowledgement of her presence in his life.

That night, Arvind slept peacefully. No restlessness, no pain, just a quiet surrender. Before closing his eyes, he murmured, "The river flows, the sun sets and the stars take their place. Everything is as should be."

The next morning as the first rays of dawn filtered through the window, Arvind took his final breath, leaving behind a legacy of knowledge, devotion and a life lived with purpose behind.

Usha bringing him back was a power, an act of love. She ensured his return home — both physically and metaphorically, before his final transition. Usha and Mukund, though grieving, found solace in his peaceful departure. Mukund took vows to continue his mission, not just as a scientist but as someone who understood the deeper connection between knowledge and the soul.

Usha, now alone dedicated herself to preserving Arvind's work and wisdom, ensuring that his name and teachings lived on.

35

As the news of Arvind's demise spread, it was like wildfire consuming hearts with grief. Scientists, spiritual seekers, students and admirers, everyone who had even the slightest connection with him were shaken.

People from all walks of life, from renowned physicists, to humble devotees started arriving at Usha's home, some came in silence, some in tears, but all with a deep sense of loss.

Inside the house, Usha sat near Arvind's still body, her eyes dry but soul burdened with an unspeakable emptiness. She was not just mourning her companion; she was witnessing the end of an era.

Mukund arrived, his heart heavy. He had known this day would come, but he still felt unprepared. He touched Arvind's feet, whispering, "I will carry forward your legacy, Sir."

Usha looked at Arvind's lifeless body, her voice trembling as she spoke, "This man… all his life, he only knew pain and misery. He never wanted anything for himself. All he ever cared about was using nuclear science for the good of humanity… and his wholehearted care for me and Mukund."

Tears welled up in her eyes as she whispered, "What have I done for him—except regret everything now?"

She knelt beside him, her hand gently resting on his chest. "Arvind, you've done everything for me. But there's still one task left. You have to bless Mukund. Let him become Arvind Junior—for me."

The tricoloured draped coffin moved slowly towards the cremation ground, a sea of people followed. The streets were overflowing; rooftop packed with people who had gathered for one last glimpse of Arvind. The solemnity of the moment was broken only by the resounding cries of the crowd.

ARVIND AMAR RAHE, ARVIND AMAR RAHE.

(Long live Arvind).

From the scientific community to spiritual seekers from students to common citizens, everyone felt the loss personally. Some held placards, with his quotes, others carried flowers and many simply stood with folded hands, eyes brimming with tears.

Inside the vehicle carrying Arvind's body, Usha sat in silence. She did not cry but her heart was heavy with the weight of loss. She looked at the man she loved, still loves and will forever love and whispered,

"Arvind, you have taught me everything, Physics, spirituality and fight against inhumanity, but you never taught me how to live without you."

The man who had been her world was now a memory — a name on people's lips.

She heard the chants, saw the sea of people and whispered to herself, "You never sought recognition, Arvind, yet the world bows before you today."

Given Arvind's contribution to science and spirituality, the government decided to honour him with a state funeral. The Prime Minister issued a statement:

> *India has lost a visionary – one who bridged the seen and the unseen, the atom and the Atma. His wisdom will guide generations to come.*

The tricolour draped coffin moved slowly towards the cremation ground. Flowers rained from balconies and rooftops as if the entire universe was mourning its beloved son. Monks recited Vedic hymns, scientists earned his unfinished research and young students vowed to continue his quest for knowledge.

Mukund, walking beside the body felt the enormity of the moment. He realised that Arvind had not just left a void; he had left a responsibility.

As the funeral pyre was prepared, the moment of Mukhagni—the sacred ritual of lighting the funeral fire—approached. The air was thick with the scent of sandalwood and the weight of unshed tears.

Mukund, standing near Arvind's body, took a deep breath, steadying himself. This was not just a ritual; it was the final act of duty, of love, of acceptance. Mukund had been a disciple, a protégé, a friend, but today, he was a son.

With trembling hands, he took the sacred flame and whispered, "Sir, I was never your blood, but you nurtured me with knowledge and love. Today I perform this duty as your son, as your legacy-bearer."

As he placed the flame on the pyre, the flames rose, engulfing Arvind's mortal remains, the chants did not die down. Instead, they grew louder, stronger, filled with emotion and conviction.

Usha closed her eyes, knowing that though his body had turned to ashes, his soul, his ideas and his spirit would forever guide the world. Usha standing beside Mukund watched the fire consume the last traces of the man who had been her world.

She did not wait, nor did she breakdown. Instead, she folded her hands and whispered softly, "Arvind, you always belonged to the universe and today the universe has taken you back."

Hours later, as the embers turned to ash, Mukund collected them with reverence. The sacred remains would be immersed in the Yamuna, completing the cycle of life and death, science and spirituality, man and eternity.

Before leaving, he turned back one last time murmuring, "You are gone, Sir, but I will ensure that your light never fades."

And with that, the son of Arvind's ideals walked into the future, carrying his legacy forward.

36

In the days following Arvind's demise, Mukund felt an immense void. The absence of his mentor was like a missing piece in his own existence. The lab, the books, the unfinished notes, everything reminded him of Arvind. For the first time, he questioned himself.

Can I truly carry forward what Arvind envisioned, or am I just a shadow of his greatness?

Usha, though grieving became a pillar of strength. She reminded Mukund, "Arvind didn't want a follower, he wanted a thinker. You must not just continue his work; you must evolve it."

This struck a chord in Mukund. He realised that his duty is not merely to replicate Arvind, but to build upon his foundation.

With renewed determination, Mukund started refining Arvind's work, merging nuclear physics with deeper philosophical inquiries. He started delivering lectures, publishing Arvind's unfinished papers and even writing a book titled, *Beyond the Atom: Arvind's Legacy of Science and Soul.*

His speeches echoed Arvind's wisdom, but with his own unique insights. He introduced innovations that Arvind dreamed but never completed. Scientists began to recognise him not just as Arvind's protégé, but as a visionary in his own right. Usha kept on reminding about Arvind's ideals.

Months after Arvind's passing, the government, recognising his unparalleled contribution to science and spirituality announced a fitting tribute. On behalf of scientists, students and the people of India, a grand monument was erected at the entrance of Bhabha Atomic Research Centre (BARC), Mumbai, the very place where his journey in nuclear physics had begun.

The structure was unlike any other, a masterpiece that embodied Arvind's dual existence. At the base, a massive stone carving of Lord Krishna, symbolising his deep-rooted spirituality.

Rising above a lowering metallic structure resembling an ATOM, representing his scientific genius. In the centre, a plaque inscribed with his most profound words:

The atom and the *atma* are not separate. Science discovers the universe; spirituality unites with it.

Usha stepped forward and gently touched the plaque. In that moment, she felt his presence not in the stone or metal but in the air.

"You always belonged to knowledge, Arvind. Now knowledge belongs to you, you are irreplaceable."

❧ ❧ ❧

Years later, standing before Arvind's memorial, Mukund whispered, "I no longer seek to fill the void you left Sir. Instead, I have let your wisdom shape me into something new. You are not gone, you live in every equation, every discovery and every heart you touched."

Standing beside his mother, Mukund clenched his fist with determination and made a promise to himself.

"This is not just a monument, this is a responsibility. I will ensure that every student who walks past it, knows Arvind's name not just as a scientist, but as a guiding force."

Arvind merged science with spirituality, and in that sacred union, his soul touched immortality.

In the quiet corners of devotion, Usha's platonic love for Arvind blossomed—eternal and unspoken.

Other Works by the Author

Love on Ventilator

Love Triology, Who to Complain

It's Ok to Fall in Love Again

The Son Rose from the West

Mohini The Tigress

Love Lost in Transit

Indu The Parched Woman

Mother Vs Surrogate: A Tale of Two Mothers

Is That Love or Fantasy?

LOVE Will That Cherish or Perish?

Rukhsaar: The Woman of Substance

Urmila: Unspoken & Unappreciated

Raghu: The Self-Made Man

Ye Hosla Kaise Ruke

VIDUR (Archer, Strategist & Mahatma)

Love From The Other World

The Flame That Still Burns (Necrogamy)

Shrutakirti (Sita's Sister)

Shrutakirti (Sita's Sister)– Hindi Version

Anmol, The Heir Apparent

Jatayu: The Divine Bird

Love Beyond Boundaries

Soulmates in Silence

ARVIND

The Mind That Couldn't Be Weaponised